Library of Congress Cataloging-in-Publication Data

Cocca-Leffler, Maryann, 1958-.
Jungle Halloween / written and illustrated by Maryann Cocca-Leffler.
p. cm.
Summary: Rhyming verses tell the story of jungle animals that decorate for
Halloween, dress up for the occasion, and participate in the night's festivities.
ISBN 0-8075-4056-0 (hardcover)
[1. Jungle animals—Fiction. 2. Halloween—Fiction. 3. Stories in rhyme.]
I. Title.
PZ8.3.C634 Ju 2000
99-050903
Text and illustrations copyright © 2000 by Maryann Cocca-Leffler.
Published in 2000 by Albert Whitman & Company, 6340 Oakton Street,
Morton Grove, Illinois 60053-2723.
Published simultaneously in Canada by General Publishing, Limited, Toronto.
Printed in the United States of America.
10 9 8 7 6 5 4 3 2 1

To my husband, Eric, who knows it's a jungle out there.

Thanks, Kristin, for wanting a jungle room!
Love, Mom

Jungle Halloween

by

Maryann Cocca-Leffler

The light is low,
the wind is still.
The Jungle has
a spooky chill.

The animals
      are out of sight,
preparing for
      a special night.

Jungle Carving

Jungle Blowing

Jungle pumpkins,
big and bright,
with Jungle faces
light the night.

Jungle Frown

Jungle Smile

It's nothing like you've ever seen...

Jungle Goblin

Jungle Clown

It's a Jungle Halloween!

The animals gather
in two long lines,
march into the swamp
and under the vines.

They stop to ask
for something sweet
and sing a chorus—

ELLA
FANT

"Trick or treat!"

Jungle Wiggle

Jungle Moo?

JUNGLE
PARK

PARTY
TONIGHT

Through the trees,
oh, so dark!
Over the hills
to Jungle Park.

It's nothing like you've ever seen...

It's a Jungle Halloween!

They sing and dance
in Jungle beat
and eat and eat
and eat and EAT!

Jungle Candy

Jungle Cake

Tired animals
under the vines
trudge slowly home
in two wobbly lines.

Jungle Scrub

Jungle Weep

Jungle Yawn

Jungle Sleep